Wildly Perfect

Written by
Brooke McMahan

Illustrated by
Ryan Kovar

For my precious girl, Danica.
You are the greatest gift life could ever give me.

Wildly Perfect

Written by
Brooke McMahan

Illustrated by
Ryan Kovar

atmosphere press

Embrace who you're becoming,
Don't water down your wild.
You're remarkably unique,
My bold and beautiful child.

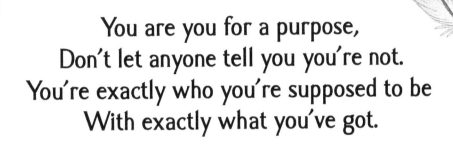

You are you for a purpose,
Don't let anyone tell you you're not.
You're exactly who you're supposed to be
With exactly what you've got.

When you fall, because you will,
Fall powerfully like the rain
With all the grace inside you
May all your strength remain.

Don't ever say you're sorry
For the person that you are.
Fly high among your dreams,
Just like a shooting star.

Keep your chin held high
No matter what they say.
Be proud of who you are
At the end of every day.

Be bold, courageous, and graceful.
Be kind, curious, and fun.
Your innocent, playful spirit
Is a gift to everyone.

If you get confused or lost,
Or can't tell right from wrong,
I'll be here to guide you
And remind you that you're strong.

You can accomplish any goal
You just need to understand,
The secret to achieving them
Is believing that you can.

The clouds can't dull your sparkle,
The dark can't dim your shine.
You are remarkably magnificent,
I'm so proud that you are mine.

ABOUT THE AUTHOR

Brooke McMahan is an author with a passion for writing books that empower children to use their voice and accept themselves exactly as they are. She is a native Oklahoman who enjoys reading, writing, bike riding and eating delicious food, but her favorite thing to do is spend time with her husband and their rambunctious little girl. Brooke attended the University of Oklahoma and received a Bachelor of Science in Communication Sciences and Disorders. She then went on to attend the University of Oklahoma Health Sciences Center and earned a Doctorate in Audiology. She currently lives in Edmond, Oklahoma where she works in neuromonitoring. She spends her days in the operating room and spends her nights creating inspiring stories to encourage children to live to their full potential.

ABOUT THE ILLUSTRATOR

Ryan Kovar is a professional artist who specializes in illustration, character design, graphic design, animation and voice-over acting. After being diagnosed with an Autism Spectrum Disorder at an early age, he turned to drawing as a way to help express what he had a difficult time expressing, verbally. After earning his associate's degree in graphic design, he went on to earn his BFA in film and animation from Rochester Institute of Technology. Post- graduation Ryan has created art for various media, including magazines, books, print advertising, short films and a cartoon series. His animated thesis film, " Hunt or Be Hunted" has been featured in multiple film festivals around the country, including New York City and California. Ryan currently lives in Rochester, New York.

ABOUT ATMOSPHERE PRESS

Atmosphere Press is an independent, full-service publisher for excellent books in all genres and for all audiences. Learn more about what we do at atmospherepress.com.

We encourage you to check out some of Atmosphere's latest releases, which are available at Amazon.com and via order from your local bookstore:

Beau Wants to Know, a picture book by Brian Sullivan

The King's Drapes, a picture book by Jocelyn Tambascio

You are the Moon, a picture book by Shana Rachel Diot

Onionhead, a picture book by Gary Ziskovsky

Odo and the Stranger, a picture book by Mark Johnson

Jack and the Lean Stalk, a picture book by Raven Howell

Brave Little Donkey, a picture book by Rachel L. Pieper

Buried Treasure: A Cool Kids Adventure, a picture book by Anne Krebbs

Young Yogi and the Mind Monsters, an illustrated retelling of Patanjali by Sonja Radvila

The Magpie and The Turtle, a picture book by Timothy Yeahquo

The Alligator Wrestler: A Girls Can Do Anything Book, children's fiction by Carmen Petro

My WILD First Day of School, a picture book by Dennis Mathew

The Sky Belongs to the Dreamers, a picture book by J.P. Hostetler

I Will Love You Forever and Always, a picture book by Sarah Thomas Mariano

Shooting Stars: A Girls Can Do Anything Book, children's fiction by Carmen Petro

Oscar the Loveable Seagull, a picture book by Mark Johnson

Carpenters and Catapults: A Girls Can Do Anything Book, children's fiction by Carmen Petro

Gone Fishing: A Girls Can Do Anything Book, children's fiction by Carmen Petro

Bello the Cello, a picture book by Dennis Mathew

That Scarlett Bacon, a picture book by Mark Johnson

CPSIA information can be obtained
at www.ICGtesting.com
Printed in the USA
BVHW020948050821
613726BV00018B/538

9 781637 528150